Walk with Me, Sawyer Bear

by

Richard Tepler

Harry
Imagination...
Dreams...
&
wonderful childhood
Memories.
Enjoy!
Richard Tepler
2018

DORRANCE PUBLISHING CO., INC.
PITTSBURGH, PENNSYLVANIA 15222

Dorrance Publishing Co., Inc.
701 Smithfield Street
Pittsburgh, PA 15222
Visit our website at *www.dorrancebookstore.com*

ISBN: 978-1-4349-1529-0
eISBN: 978-1-4349-1541-2

To Don and Kathy, thank you for sharing a part of your life with me.
And to all of you who have touched my life in some way, especially my children:
Christopher, Jill, and Marena.
You have not only touched my life but also my heart.
And especially for my grandson, Sawyer Bear. May your life be filled with joy and
happiness. Grandpa loves you.

To Mrs. S. and Mrs. H., thanks for your inspiration and encouragement to write.
I haven't forgotten.

April Rain

Showers of April rain
racing down the windowpane.
Oh, that lovely
April rain.

Showers of April rain
falling on the field of brown.
Oh, that lovely April rain
soaking in the ground.

Showers of April rain
melting leftover winter snow.
Oh, that lovely April rain
that races down the window pane
and
soaks into the winter ground
melting snow all around.

Kites

Kites with string
climbing up high.
Dancing in March
against a cold blue sky.

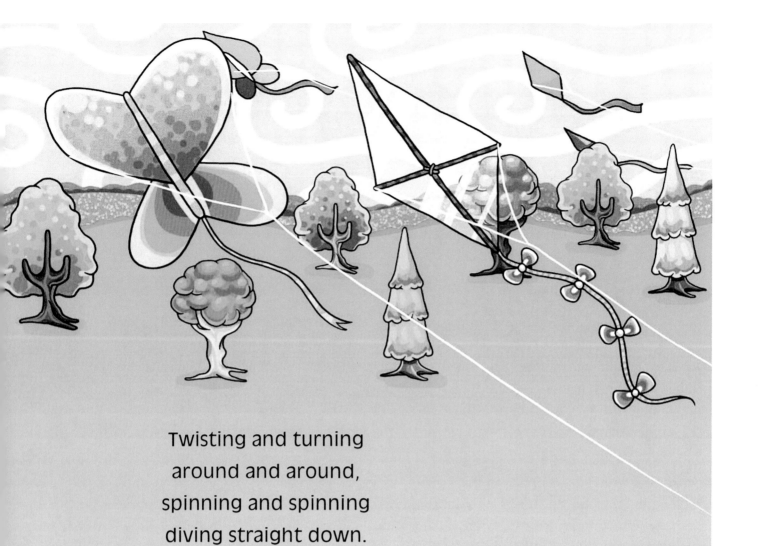

Twisting and turning
around and around,
spinning and spinning
diving straight down.

Faster and faster
away from the sky,
smacking the ground
with a kite-breaking sound.

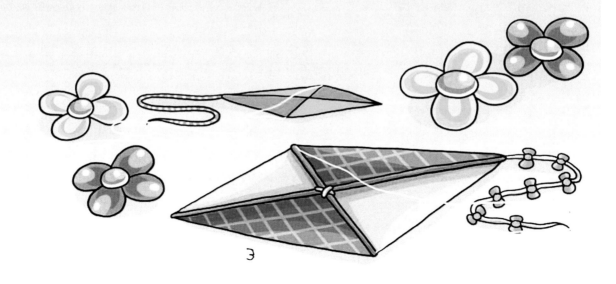

3

I Went to the Park

I went to the park
with my mom, my dad, and my bear.
I went to the park
to see what was there.

Children were laughing
and having some fun.
Children were yelling
and trying to run.

Dad was pushing
the merry-go-round.
Sis was dragging
her feet on the ground.

4

Mom was pushing
the swing up high.
My feet were reaching
up to the sky.

I went to the park
to see what was there.
But
my favorite things
were
my mom, my dad, and my bear.

Summertime Fun

Summertime fun
in the summertime sun,
feel the warmth
of
the summer sun.

Summertime noise
from summertime boys,
playing games
with summertime toys.

Summer Day Wind

Clouds on a summer day—
here comes the wind, pushing them
away.

Trees on a summer day—
along comes the wind, making them
sway.

Flowers on a summer day—
feel the wind and watch them play.

Children on a summer day—
Don't let the wind blow you away!

Bugs

Bugs in June
under a summer moon,
busy at night
and
sleeping 'til noon.

Bugs in July
I wonder why
the mosquitoes bite
and flies fly.

8

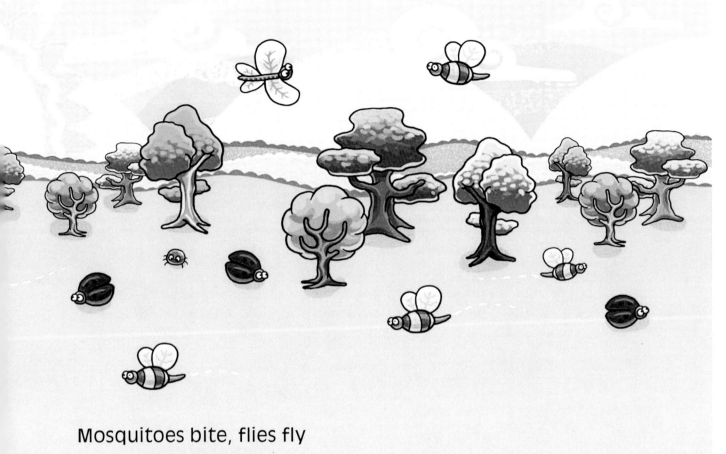

Mosquitoes bite, flies fly
chasing each other
in July.

Bugs in August
please go away,
it's much too hot
for you to stay.

Bugs under the summer sun,
chasing each other
and
having summer fun.

The Airplane

You know...
While you were flying overhead,
I heard the roar,
jumped out of bed.

While you are scraping
skies of blue.
I am looking up at you.

And when you disappear
from sight,
racing past
the morning light.

I will wonder from below
Just how far
you can go.

I'll wonder how you stay so
long
up in the sky
where you belong.

The Bridge

Reach across
and touch the sides.
Stretch yourself
and open wide.

Hold the cars,
the trucks,
the bus,
and keep the water
under us.

Hold me up
as I walk along.
How you must be very strong

to keep the cars,
the trucks,
and bus
from falling down
from under us.

13

14

Leaf

The prettiest leaf
I ever found,

Lying right there
on the ground.

Yellow, orange,
and
splashes of red.

A million more
above my head.

15

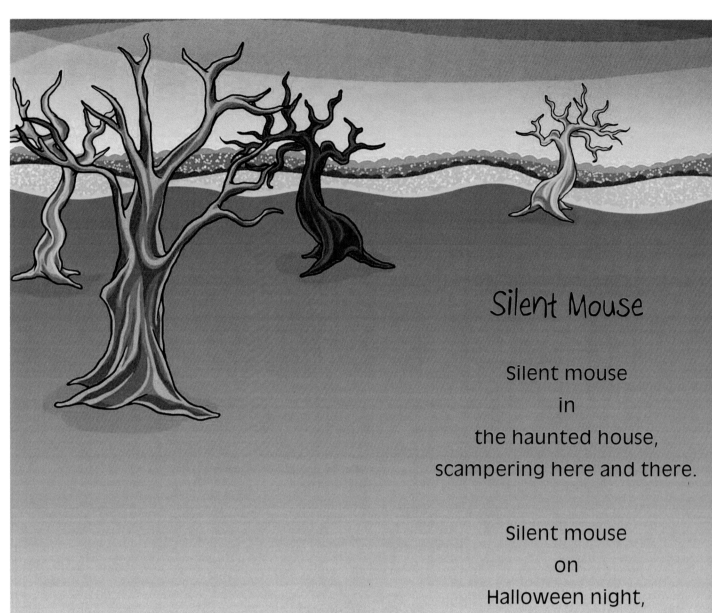

Silent Mouse

Silent mouse
in
the haunted house,
scampering here and there.

Silent mouse
on
Halloween night,
scaring the children
with Halloween fright.

Silent mouse
in
the haunted house
watching the flying bat.

Oh, silent mouse
in
the haunted house,

WATCH OUT!
For silent cat.

Halloween Night

Into the night
the goblins walk,
the bats will fly
and the wind will talk.
OOOHHH went the wind.

Into the night
the skeletons creak,
the ghost will moan
and the witch will shriek.
EEEKKK went the witch.

Into the night
trick-or-treaters stroll,
strange things happen
wherever they go.

November's Trees

November's trees
are bare.
Scattered leaves
are everywhere.
Burning smells
are in the air.
November's trees
are bare.
Scattered leaves
are everywhere.

20

Winter

Winter cold
ice and snow,
covers up
the autumn leaves.

Winter white
blowing cold,
walk along
on
crunchy snow.

January Snow

Cold winter wind
blowing over white fields
of January snow.

Blowing cold
against a warm face,
while walking through white fields
of January snow.

Pushing snow
against heavy boots,
as cold winter wind
blows over white fields
of January snow.

It's Cold Outside

Red mittens, green mittens,
Brown mittens, blue.
Mittens with holes
and
some that are new.

Black boots, red boots,
yellow boots, too.
Boots with zippers
go over my shoes.

Red scarf, green scarf,
brown scarf, blue.
My scarf is long
to
wrap around you.

25

After February

March winds
blowing cold,
Sunny skies
on
old winter snow.

Brown patches
of
summer grass,
lazy sleds
of winter past.

My Mother

This is my mother
so pretty and fair.

This is my mother
with beautiful hair.

I love my mother.
Can't you see?

When I hug my mother
she hugs me.

28

My Daddy

My daddy is tall
and very smart.

My daddy loves me
with all his heart.

My daddy will hug
and squeeze me tight.

My daddy can make
everything all right.

My daddy is special
as you can see.

I love my daddy
and he loves me.

29

Throughout the Year

Springtime rain
from stormy clouds,
thunder laughing,
cracking loud.

Summertime games
oh, what fun,
swimming under
the summer sun.

Autumn leaves falling
from sleepy trees,
dancing in
the autumn breeze.

Wintertime white
ice and snow,
cover up
your freezing nose.

31

Best Friends

I've got brown eyes,
you have blue.

I've got new shoes,
and new socks, too.

I've got blue pants,
you have green.

I've got knee socks,
under my blue jeans.

I've got friends,
so do you.

We're best friends
whatever we do.